Dear Parent:

Psst . . . you're looking at the Super ~~~~ of Reading. It's called comics.

STEP INTO READING® COMIC READERS are a perfect step in learning to read. They provide visual cues to the meaning of words and helpfully break out short pieces of dialogue into speech balloons.

Here are some terms commonly associated with comics:
  PANEL: A section of a comic with a box drawn around it.
  CAPTION: Narration that helps set the scene.
  SPEECH BALLOON: A bubble containing dialogue.
  GUTTER: The space between panels.

Tips for reading comics with your child:

- Have your child read the speech balloons while you read the captions.
- Ask your child: What is a character feeling? How can you tell?
- Have your child draw a comic showing what happens after the book is finished.

STEP INTO READING® COMIC READERS are designed to engage and to provide an empowering reading experience. They are also fun. The best-kept secret of comics is that they create lifelong readers. And that will make you the real hero of the story!

Jenn — M. Holm

Jennifer L. Holm and Matthew Holm
Co-creators of the Babymouse and Squish series

For Cooper

Step into Reading, Random House, and the Random House colophon are registered trademarks of Penguin Random House LLC.

Visit us on the Web!
StepIntoReading.com
rhcbooks.com

Educators and librarians, for a variety of teaching tools, visit us at RHTeachersLibrarians.com

ISBN 978-0-593-12789-6 (trade) — ISBN 978-0-593-12790-2 (lib. bdg.)

Printed in the United States of America
10 9 8 7 6 5 4 3 2 1

SANTIAGO OF THE SEAS

SEARCH FOR THE SPYGLASS

by Melissa Lagonegro

based on the episode "The Magic Spyglass" by Leslie Valdes

illustrated by Marcela Cespedes-Alicea

Random House 🏠 New York

Santiago, Lorelai, and Tomás are playing Pirate I Spy.

Santiago is afraid of spiders!

He drops the spyglass.

The spyglass breaks!

Maybe Abuelo can fix it.

I am sorry. It is broken.

The compass shows them something!

A Magic Spyglass!
It has special powers.

It is hidden in Skull Mountain.
The pirates must find it!

The greedy pirate Enrique sees them.

A Magic Spyglass? I want it!

The good pirates make it to Skull Mountain. They enter a cave.

Yikes! More spiders!

They find the Magic Spyglass!

We can use it to help people!

They also find booby traps.

Santiago finds a way over.

Step on the lights!

Enrique tries to take the Magic Spyglass.

Rocks fall!

I am out of here!

Enrique escapes.
The others are trapped!

The Magic Spyglass can see through walls!

The wall is fake. It leads to a tunnel.

20

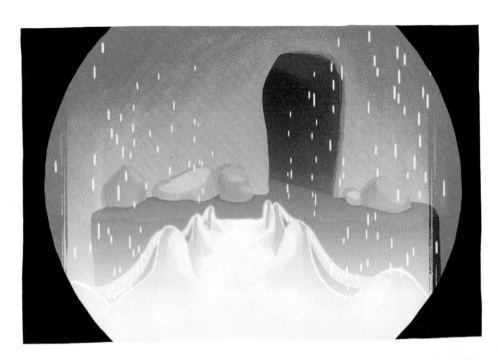

They see an invisible bridge.

Kiko stops Enrique.

Enrique falls into a trap.

Yikes! Spiderwebs!

26

Enrique drops the Magic Spyglass.
Santiago needs it to find a way out!

Kiko grabs the Magic
Spyglass with his tongue.

It has night vision!

Santiago sees a giant spiderweb!

They use the bouncy web to jump out.

Enrique runs away.

Argh!

The night vision guides the good pirates home.